It's a dog's life

Mark Stern

Jonathan Cape

Thirty Bedford Square London

To Angela Littler,
who made this book possible

From Aunty Vera
for Ella's second birthday

First published 1978
© 1978 by Mark Stern
Jonathan Cape Ltd, 30 Bedford Square, London WC1

British Library Cataloguing in Publication Data
Stern, Mark
   It's a dog's life.
   1. Title
   823'. 9' 1J   PZ10.3
ISBN   0-224-01568-0

Printed in Great Britain by Sackville Press Billericay Ltd.

Patch came from a large family. They were not at all rich but they were very happy.

These are Patch's parents.

Here are Patch and Honey (his shy, loving and faithful girlfriend).

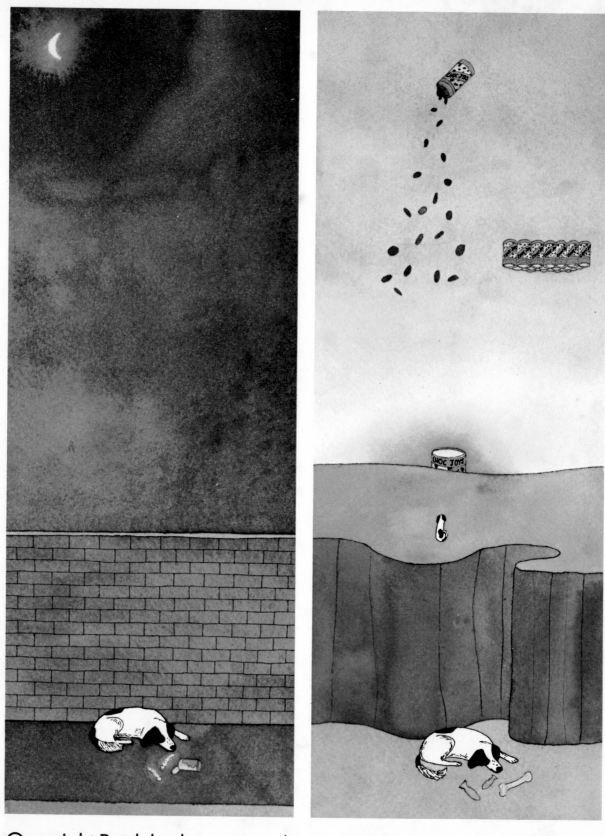

One night Patch had a strange dream. He dreamt up Choc Joys.

Then he remembered an advertisement he had seen. By morning he
realized how he could make his fortune.

He decided to take his idea to Bulldog Foods Ltd and set off to the Big City. Because he knew he had a long way to go he began to run.

All through the night he ran and ran. By dawn, tired and hungry, he was nearing the Big City. When he arrived at the offices of Bulldog Foods Ltd, Patch completely forgot his hunger and exhaustion.

The offices of the Chairman, Bulldog Major, were on the top floo

So Patch took the lift.

Patch waited anxiously before being shown into Bulldog Major's office. He liked Patch's idea and after long discussions Patch happily signed a contract. Outside, Honey, who had secretly followed Patch, had got lost at a corner.

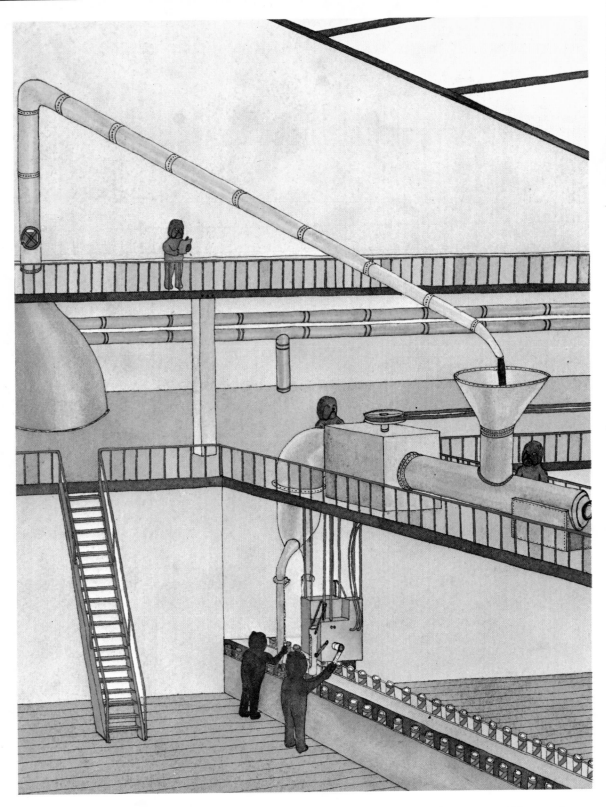

A large new factory was built specially to manufacture Choc Joys.

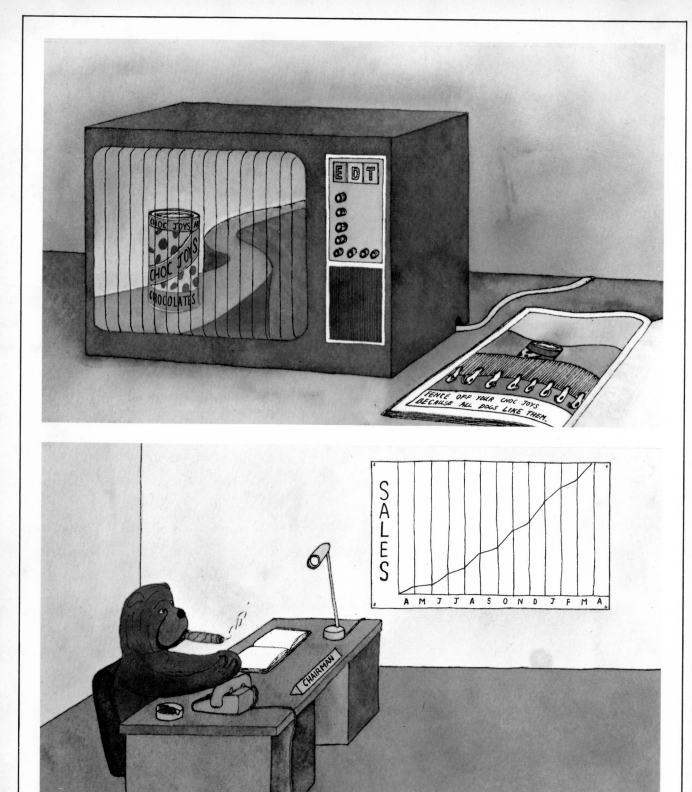

There was a massive advertising campaign to launch Choc Joys. The new product became a great success. Bulldog Major was happy as sales soared.

Because of the huge demand for Choc Joys bulk transport had to be introduced. Honey, who still had not found Patch, was living rough.

Bulldog Major became very rich and he bought a grand country mansion, set among trees and lawns and surrounded by high walls and strong gates. He made Patch live in the mansion so he could keep an eye on him.

Patch was given a large new desk and a bright red telephone. Then he was tied to the desk with a heavy iron chain and expected to work harder than ever planning new sales campaigns.

Bulldog Major lived like a king in this house which crawled with his servants.

Patch on the other hand was a prisoner, worked to the bone, chained to his desk and watched by guards. Bulldog Major soon had a large limousine and a private jet. Bulldog Foods Ltd became Bulldog Enterprises Inc.

Bulldog Enterprises Inc. acquired a new prestige office block. It was many storeys high and stood in the expensive part of town near the park.

Honey finally discovered where Patch was living and hurried to rejoin him.

But when she asked to see Patch, the door was slammed in her face.

When Patch learned about this, he was very angry and he firmly refused to work any more. So Bulldog Major sent for him and sacked him without a moment's hesitation, thinking he no longer needed Patch anyway.

Patch was thrown out of the house without a penny. For a while he was very sad but then he found Honey and raced to her, happy once again.

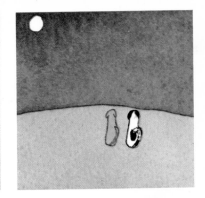

They ran together completely carefree, rediscovering the true joys of life: fresh air, grass and trees. They ran well into the night until they were far from any Bulldogs.

They found a little stone cottage and settled down to a happy quiet life in the country.